TWITCH AND THE INVISIBLE WIND

AN OWLEGORIES TALE

CREATED BY THOMAS AND JULIE BOTO

ILLUSTRATED BY ANDREA WERNTZ

Twitch was a wild and wacky owl.

He liked to run fast and fly high.

There was just one problem.

Twitch had a bad crash.
And now he was afraid to fly.

All his owl friends could fly.

They zoomed up and down.

They did flips and loops.

Twitch wanted to fly again
more than anything.

But Twitch was worried
he might crash again.

Twitch's friend Nora saw
his sad face.

"What's wrong, Twitch?"
she asked.

Twitch muttered.

"Oh," said Nora. "You're scared. That's okay, Twitch. I used to be afraid to fly too."

"But God made us with wings that are just right for flying," Nora explained.

Twitch nodded.

But he still didn't try to fly.

"When we flap our wings," Nora said,
"The air pressure lifts us up."

Twitch nodded.

But he still didn't try to fly.

"When we're up in the sky, the
wind currents help us soar!"
Nora called.

"Just spread your wings and let
the wind do all the work!"

Twitch nodded.

But he still didn't try to fly.

"Are you worried, Twitch?"
Nora asked.

Twitch twittered. He squawked and
screeched and skittered.

"I understand, Twitch," said Nora.
"You're not sure how to trust the wind
when you can't see it."

"Eek!" Twitch squeeked.

"Maybe I can help," said Nora.

"Even though you can't see the wind,
you still know it's there." Nora said.

"Look at those trees, Twitch. See how they're bending in the wind?"

Twitch looked at the trees.

He'd never really noticed them sway before.

But he still didn't try to fly.

"Look at those leaves on the ground.
See how the wind is blowing them?"

Twitch looked at the leaves.

He could see the wind making them flutter and float.

But he still didn't try to fly.

Nora looked at Twitch. "You know Twitch, sometimes I wonder if God is with me. Then I remember that even though I can't see God, I can see all the things God does. The wind reminds me of God. It's always there. Even if I can't see it."

Twitch thought about beautiful
flowers that bloomed in the spring.

He thought about his parents and
how much they loved him.

He thought about his friends and
how kind they were to him.

These were all good things God had
given him. They helped him see God.

Suddenly, Nora turned to Twitch
with a bright look in her eyes.

"Twitch, look at your wings!"

Twitch looked down.

His feathers were
blowing in the breeze.

The wind felt cool.

The wind tickled.

He could *feel* the wind.

The wind was there!

"Come on Twitch, you've got
to try it!" Nora said.

Twitch stood. Twitch thought.
Twitch closed his eyes and felt
the wind ruffle his feathers.

And then Twitch ran as fast he could!
He flapped his wings and closed his eyes.

And the wind carried him

right up

to the sky.

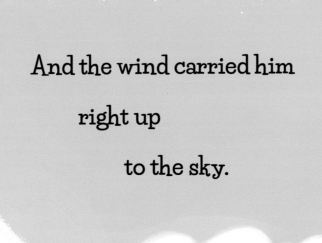

FAMILY TIME

"The wind blows wherever it pleases. You hear its sound, but you cannot tell where it comes from or where it is going. So it is with everyone born of the Spirit." — John 3:8 (NIV)

TALK ABOUT THE STORY:

> The Bible says God made a wind to pass over the earth.

> It blows and blows wherever it pleases and we cannot see it.

> Even though we can't see the wind, we still know it's there.

> We can feel the wind. We can see all the things the wind does.

> God is with us all the time. We can't see God, but we can see all the good things God does.

What are some of the good things God has given you?

Pray Together:

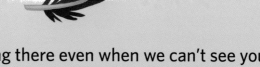

Thank you, God, for being there even when we can't see you. Help us keep our eyes open to all the ways you show us your love and care. Amen.

Make Something:

1. Cut a square out of brightly colored paper.

2. Cut a line from each corner toward the center of the square, stopping about one inch from the center.

3. Pull every other corner toward the center, curling the paper, not folding.

4. Secure these corners to the center of the paper with a straight pin.

5. Poke the pin through a pencil eraser and fold the end of the pin down.

You have made a pinwheel! Take it outside to see how it moves when the wind blows.

While you're outside, look for other ways you see the wind at work!

The Owlegories® brand and characters are the property of Spy House, LLC.

Created by Thomas and Julie Boto
Illustrated by Andrea Werntz
Designed by Mighty Media

First edition published 2017
Printed in the United States of America
23 22 21 20 19 18 17   1 2 3 4 5 6 7 8

ISBN: 9781506433059

Library of Congress Cataloging-in-Publication Data

Names: Boto, Thomas, author. | Boto, Julie, author. | Werntz, Andrea
    (Illustrator), illustrator.
Title: Twitch and the invisible wind : an owlegories tale / created by Thomas
    and Julie Boto ; illustrated by Andrea Werntz.
Description: First edition. | Minneapolis, MN : Sparkhouse Family, 2017. |
    Summary: Twitch the owl is afraid to fly after a big crash, but his
    friend, Nora, reminds him that wind will help even though, like God, it
    cannot be seen directly. Includes "Family time" suggestions for
    discussion, prayer, and a craft.
Identifiers: LCCN 2017025934 | ISBN 9781506433059
Subjects: | CYAC: Flight--Fiction. | Fear--Fiction. | Owls--Fiction. |
    Faith--Fiction. | Christian life--Fiction.
Classification: LCC PZ7.1.B676 Twi 2017 | DDC [E]--dc23 LC record available
at https://lccn.loc.gov/2017025934

VN0003466; 9781506433059; JUL2017

Sparkhouse Family
510 Marquette Avenue
Minneapolis, MN 55402
sparkhouse.org